Ramadan and Id al-Fitr

Dianne M. MacMillan

Reading Consultant:

Michael P. French, Ph.D.
Bowling Green State University

—Best Holiday Books—

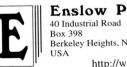

Enslow Publishers, Inc.

40 Industrial Road
Box 398
Berkeley Heights, NJ 07922
USA

PO Box 38
Aldershot
Hants GU12 6BP
UK

http://www.enslow.com

Acknowledgments

The author wishes to thank Dr. Frank Peters, professor of religion at New York University, and Dr. Muzammil H. Siddiqi, religious director of the Islamic Society of Orange County (Ca.) for their careful reading of the manuscript; and Dr. Aman Attieh, lecturer in Arabic languages, University of Texas, Austin, for her review of the Arabic language and pronunciations used in the text.

Library of Congress Cataloging-in-Publication Data

MacMillan, Dianne.
    Ramadan and Id al-Fitr / Dianne M. MacMillan.
        p. cm. — (Best holiday books)
    Includes index.
    ISBN 0-89490-502-3
    1. Ramadan—Juvenile literature. 2. Id al-Fitr—Juvenile literature.
    3. Islam—Rituals—Juvenile literature. I. Title. II. Series.
    BP186.4.M27 1994
    297'.36—dc20   93-46185
                                                             CIP
                                                             AC

Printed in the United States of America

10 9 8

Illustration Credits: AP/Wide World Photos, pp. 11, 23; Bill Kamin, p. 17; © 1973 Diane C. Lyell, pp. 8, 39; Dianne M. MacMillan, pp. 12, 25, 29, 34; ©D.J. Lambrecht, pp. 14, 18, 21, 26, 30, 32, 41; Usamah Amer, p. 4.

Cover Illustration: © D.J. Lambrecht

Contents

This family eats an early morning breakfast during the month of Ramadan. They believe in the religion of Islam.

Breakfast Before Dawn

In many homes across the United States, families wake up while it is still dark outside. They gather in the kitchen to eat an early morning breakfast. The table is filled with plates of delicious food. It is several hours before the children leave for school. Everyone talks and laughs. Outside the last stars and the moon are visible. Why are these families eating so early?

This early morning breakfast is called suhur (su-HOOR). These families believe in the religion called Islam (is-LAHM). They are getting ready for a day without food or water. This will be their last meal until sunset.

This is Ramadan (ra-ma-DAHN). It is the

ninth month of the Islamic calendar. It is also a holiday that lasts almost thirty days. When it is over, everyone will join in a joyous festival called Id al-Fitr (EED-il-FITR). These special days are celebrated by people all over the world who follow the Islamic religion.

Muhammad

People who follow the religion of Islam are called Muslims (MUS-limz). It is a very old religion. The word Islam means "submission to the will of God." It began with a man named Muhammad (mu-HAM-mad). Muhammad was a prophet. A prophet is a special person who tells others messages from God.

Muhammad was born in the year A.D. 570 in the city of Mecca (MAK-ka) in Arabia. Today this is in the country of Saudi Arabia. The people who lived in Arabia were called Arabs. Muhammad's parents died when he was young. He was raised by his grandfather and later by an uncle.

Mecca was a trade center in the desert. Long

lines of camels carried goods and spices across the desert. These were called caravans. Caravans came from Egypt, Persia, and Syria. All of the trade routes passed through Mecca. The Arab people believed in many gods and

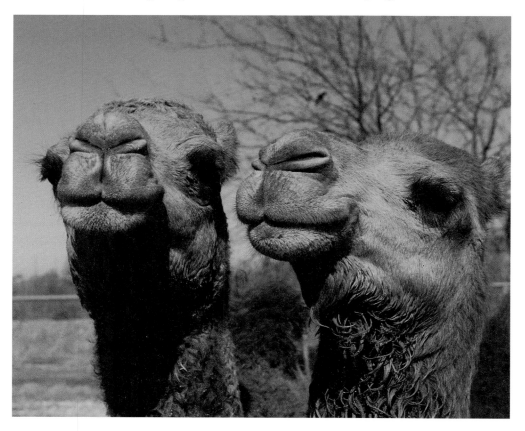

Long lines of camels carried goods and spices across the desert during the time of Muhammad. These were called caravans.

spirits. Statues and shrines were built in Mecca. People came from different places to trade and to pray before these statues.

The most important shrine was the Kaaba (KAH-bah). It was a cubelike building with a black stone built into one corner. The Arab people believed that it was built by their ancestor Abraham many centuries before. (An ancestor is a family member who is no longer living.)

Muhammad grew up and became a caravan leader. When he was forty years old, he had a vision. In his vision, the angel Gabriel told him that he must preach the word of God. [The Arabic word for God is Allah (al-LAH).] For the next few years, Muhammad had many visions from the angel. He could not read or write, so he memorized the words spoken to him. Then Muhammad spoke the words exactly as he received them. Some of his followers wrote the words down. The words were gathered together to make a book called the Koran (ko-RAHN).

At first only his family believed that his messages were from God. But slowly more people began to accept his teaching. For the next twelve years, Muhammad preached to everyone that there was only one God. He told the people they had to stop praying to the other gods. This angered the leaders of Mecca. They were afraid they might lose business if people stopped coming to pray to all the other gods. Many leaders wanted to kill Muhammad.

Finally Muhammad and his followers were forced to leave Mecca. They escaped to the city of Medina. This escape (or flight) is called the Hegira (he-JIH-rah). It took place in the year A.D. 622. This date was so important that it became the first year of the Muslim calendar.

Many people in Medina accepted Muhammad as a prophet. Muhammad felt certain that he was following the will of God. He formed an army and his power grew. In the year 630, his army of 10,000 men marched on

This is the Kaaba in the city of Mecca. Muslims face Mecca and the Kaaba when they pray.

Mecca. The people of Mecca opened their gates and accepted the new religion of Islam.

Muhammad destroyed all the shrines and statues of the other gods. But he did not destroy the Kaaba. Instead he kissed the black stone. This became a holy place. And since that time,

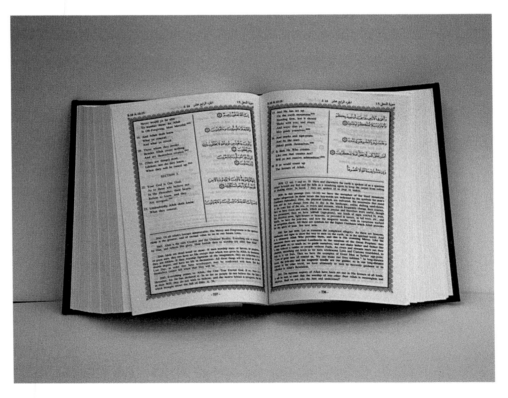

The words of Muhammad were written down by some of his followers. They were gathered together to make the Koran.

all Muslims face Mecca and the Kaaba when praying.

Muhammad died two years later at the age of sixty-two. Within 100 years of his death, the Islamic religion had spread all across the continent. It stretched from the Atlantic Ocean to the borders of China.

Today Islam is the second largest religion in the world. There are over one billion followers. In fifty-seven countries, most of the people are Muslims. Many of these countries are in the Middle East, North Africa, and Southeast Asia. There are over two and one-half million Muslims in the United States and Canada.

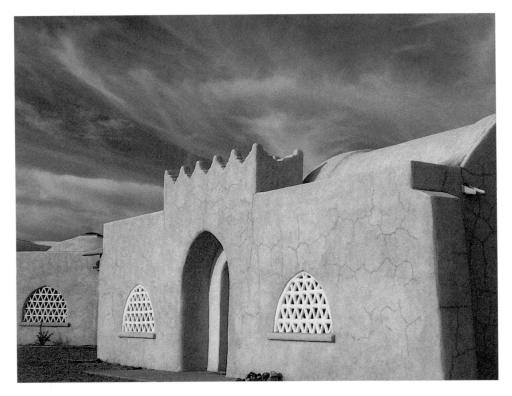

Muslims pray five times a day. Often they gather for prayer in a building like this called a mosque.

The Pillars of Islam

The Islamic faith is simple. It is founded on five duties (or rules). These rules are called the "Pillars of Islam." Children are taught the duties as soon as they are old enough to understand.

The first rule is called the shahadah (sha-HAH-dah). This means to say and believe "There is no God but Allah and Muhammad is the Messenger of Allah." Muslims say this many times every day.

The second rule is called the salat (sa-LAHT). This means daily prayer. Muslims pray five times a day in a building called a mosque (MOSK). (Mosque means "place of kneeling.") Prayers are said at dawn, at midday, at mid-afternoon, in the evening, and before bed. Before praying

Muslims remove their shoes and wash. Muslims always face in the direction of Mecca, the holy city, when praying. Muslims in the United States and Canada always face east.

The third duty is called zakat (za-KAHT). This means to give money to the poor. Every Muslim is called to help those who have less in any way they can.

The fourth rule is the fast of Ramadan. To fast means that all healthy Muslims over the age of twelve go without food or water from dawn to sunset during the month of Ramadan. Children under the age of twelve are encouraged to fast for a day several times during the month.

The fifth duty of a Muslim is to make a pilgrimage to the city of Mecca once in his or her lifetime. (A pilgrimage is a journey.) People who go on the journey are called pilgrims. This pilgrimage is called the hajj (HADJ). While on the pilgrimage, they wear special clothes. They also have certain prayers and ceremonies. As many as two million Muslims travel each year to Mecca.

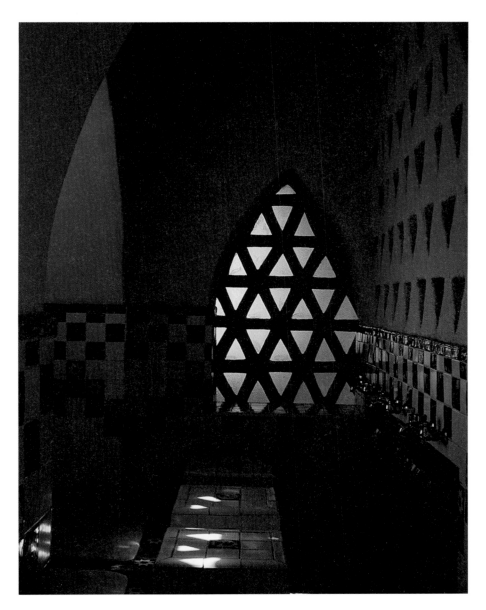

Before praying Muslims wash their hands, face, arms, and feet in a special way. This is the wash room in a mosque.

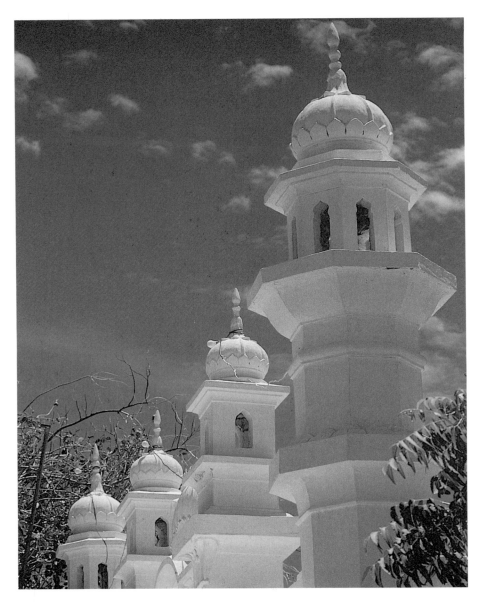

The tall tower on a mosque is called a minaret.

Mosques, Minarets, and the Koran

Mosques are important to Muslims. They usually have a high dome and at least one tower. Larger mosques have several towers. The tall tower is called a minaret. Long ago a man called a muezzin (moo-EZ-zin) would climb the tower and call the people to prayer. Today most mosques use loudspeakers with recorded messages.

Inside the mosque is a large open room. There are no altars, furniture, or chairs. People stand and then kneel on the floor when praying. The floors are often covered with beautiful carpets. People also use prayer mats.

At one end of the building is a small alcove.

This is called the mihrab (mih-RAHB). It lets people know the direction of Mecca. Everyone faces towards it. Men cover their heads as a sign of respect to God. The person who leads the prayers is called an imam (ee-MAHM). Each prayer time lasts about ten minutes. Prayers are always said in Arabic.

Women and girls pray separately from the men and boys when they come to the mosque. Most often the women say their prayers at home.

There is also a staircase that leads to a small platform. This is called the minbar (MIN-bar). On Fridays, Muslim men are expected to go to the mosque for midday prayers. After prayers, someone preaches from the minbar.

There can be no pictures of living things in the mosque. In this way the believers will think only of God. But the walls and ceilings are often decorated with verses from the Koran. They are written in beautiful writing called calligraphy. Designs are used on tiles that also cover the walls.

On Fridays Muslim men are expected to go to the mosque for midday prayers.

Before entering a mosque, Muslims remove their shoes. They wash their hands, face, arms, and feet in a special way. Mosques have large fountains in a courtyard for the washing. Prayers are said in the same way in the mosque as they would be at home or elsewhere. At home, shoes are removed and washing is done before prayers.

It is a custom that women and girls over the age of twelve dress modestly and cover their heads when they are out in public. The scarves they wear around their heads and shoulders are called hijabs (hi-JAHBS). Some Muslim-American women and girls wear hijabs. Others wear them only for religious events. Others do not follow the custom at all.

The Koran is a holy book. All of the words that the angel told Muhammad are written in the Koran. The words are in the Arabic language. The Koran has been translated into other languages, like English. However, Muslims

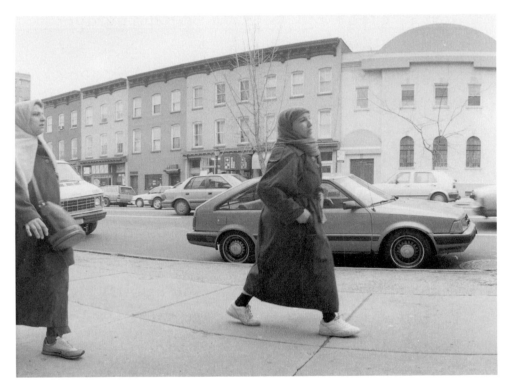

These women are walking to a mosque in New York City. It is a custom that women and girls dress modestly.

believe that if the words are not in Arabic, they do not have the same power.

For this reason, all Muslims try to learn to read Arabic. The Arabic language is read from right to left. When the Koran is read out loud, the words are chanted.

Muslim men and women cover their heads while reading the Koran. This is a sign of respect. The Koran cannot ever touch the ground or get dirty. Muslims keep it covered with cloth when they are not using it.

The Koran has 114 chapters called suras (SOO-rahs). Muslims try to memorize as many verses as they can. This takes many years of study because there are over 6,000 verses. If someone memorizes the entire Koran, the person is called a Hafiz (HAH-fiz). The family has a huge party, and everyone celebrates.

Children learn to read the Koran from start to finish. In the United States, Muslim children may attend an Islamic school. They learn about their religion and other school subjects. Others go to Saturday school held at a mosque or at an Islamic center. They learn to read and write Arabic. Most mosques have Koran schools for adults and children.

The Koran tells Muslims how to live. It teaches Muslims to be kind and loving. It tells them to trust in God at all times. The Koran has some of the same stories found in the Old and

The Koran has 114 chapters. Muslims try to memorize as many verses as they can.

New Testament of the Bible. There are stories about Adam, Noah, Abraham, Moses, and Jesus. Some Muslims carry a copy of the Koran with them wherever they go.

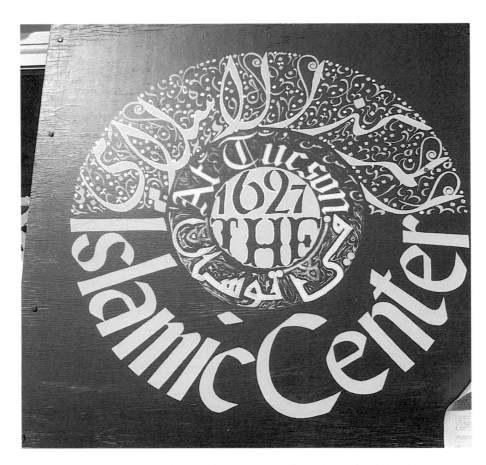

Many Muslim-American children go to Saturday school held at a mosque or at an Islamic center.

Ramadan

Muslims look forward to Ramadan. The Islamic calendar is based on the moon. The Muslim day begins at sunset, and each new month begins with the appearance of a new moon. Each month is twenty-nine or thirty days long. The lunar year is 354 days. That means that the Muslim year is ten to eleven days shorter than the solar year. The date for Ramadan changes every year. Ramadan is always the ninth month of the Islamic calendar. But it can occur in any season.

In Muslim countries, people wait with excitement for the first sight of the new moon that begins Ramadan. They climb rooftops or hills or go out into the desert. As soon as the moon is seen, people share good wishes with one another. Children greet their parents and grandparents. They kiss their hands as a sign of respect. The families go home to prepare for prayers and the early morning meal.

In other countries, the news of the moon is broadcast on radio and television. In olden days, people fired a cannon when the moon was seen.

People who are very old or sick or mothers who are nursing babies do not have to fast. But they must fast at some other time when they are able. If they cannot fast, they are asked to feed a poor person instead.

Muslims fast because they believe that God asked them to do so. By fasting they feel they become stronger in their faith. They also learn how poor people feel when they do not have enough food to eat.

Each morning the family rises early. They eat their breakfast (or suhur). If Ramadan falls in the winter when days are shorter, the meal will be light. If it is in summertime and there are

Muslims try to read the Koran from start to finish at least once during Ramadan.

many hours before sunset, then the meal will be much larger. After breakfast the family gets ready for prayers either at home or at the mosque.

At sunset Muslims break their fast with a glass of water or by eating a few dates. This is what the prophet Muhammad did. Everyone leaves the table to pray. When prayers are over, they return to enjoy a wonderful meal. The meal at sunset is called iftar (if-TAHR). Different foods are cooked at home or bought at a store.

After breakfast during Ramadan, Muslim families get ready for prayers either at home or at the mosque.

Long ago people would listen for the call from the minaret (MI-nar-ret) of the mosque to know when it was sunset. Today, in large cities in the United States, the time is announced on the radio or television. The time of sunset is also listed in newspapers. In other areas, people telephone the mosque or Islamic center.

Muslims try to read the Koran from start to finish at least once during Ramadan. They spend more time in prayer. They try hard not to quarrel or use bad words. Everyone tries to be cheerful and kind.

During Ramadan there are few activities planned during the day. In Muslim countries, restaurants are closed. Everyone waits until evening. When night arrives, mosques are lit, and restaurants and amusement parks are open. There is visiting and shopping.

The twenty-seventh night of Ramadan is called the Night of Power. Muslims believe that this is when the Koran was first given to

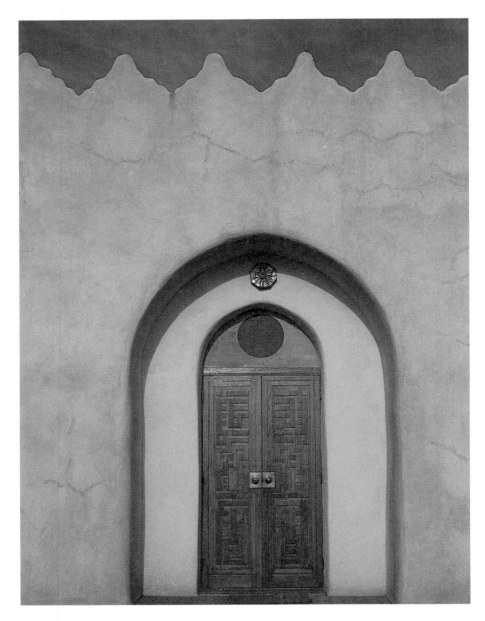

The Koran is a holy book. Walls and ceilings in mosques are often decorated with verses from this book.

Muhammad. Because they are not totally sure of the exact night, some Muslims spend the last ten nights of Ramadan in prayer.

Many Muslims believe that the last ten nights of Ramadan are holy. They believe that during these nights angels come down to earth and bless everyone.

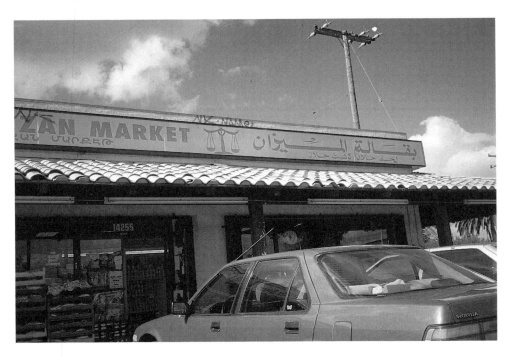

Families buy gifts and food for Id al-Fitr. This Islamic store has Arabic writing on the sign.

Preparing for Id al-Fitr

"Id" is an Arabic word. It means "a festival of happiness and a time of great joy." Id al-Fitr marks the end of the fast of Ramadan. The last week of Ramadan people prepare for Id al-Fitr. Cards are sent to neighbors, friends, and relatives.

Muslims give to the poor all during the year. But they are asked to give even more during Ramadan. The money is collected and given away a few days before Id. In this way, poor families have money to buy gifts and food for the celebration. Rich Muslim countries collect money and send it to the poorer Muslim countries.

Children grow more excited as the month of

Ramadan draws to a close. They try to guess what gifts they will receive. Will there be new clothes, shoes, or toys? But one gift is certain. They will receive lots of candy. Everyone gives candy of all kinds to the children.

Adults also look forward to the new clothes and celebrations. Houses are cleaned and painted. Then they are decorated with flowers and banners. The mosques are also decorated with flowers. The thirty days of Ramadan are almost over.

Id al-Fitr

Id al-Fitr marks the end of the fast of Ramadan. It is celebrated on the first day of the tenth month. The celebrations begin as soon as the new moon is sighted. Children and adults greet their elders by kissing their hands. Then everyone rushes to congratulate each other.

On the morning of Id al-Fitr, everyone wakes up early. They take showers or baths and put on their best clothes. Many wear perfume. They have breakfast. Then everyone goes to prayers. Prayers are held in large open spaces like parks and playgrounds. The whole Islamic community comes together. Women and children are also encouraged to come to prayers.

There are special prayers of thanksgiving.

Muslims thank God for giving them the month of Ramadan. They thank God for their faith and for giving them the Koran.

When prayers are over, men, women, and children hug each other. Everyone says, "Id Mubarak," (EED mu-BAH-rak) which means "Happy Id." The children receive clothes, toys, and candy.

In the United States, many Muslim communities have Id carnivals. There are rides and games for the children. Big balloons with the words "Happy Id" float everywhere. Adults greet one another by saying, "May Allah accept your prayers and fast of Ramadan."

The day is filled with visiting. Many families leave their doors open. People from the neighborhood go from house to house visiting. In each home, they hug and congratulate one another on the fast of Ramadan. Trays of candy and sweets are on the tables for the guests.

Id is a time to forgive one another. Family members who live far away try to come home

In the United States many Muslim communities have Id carnivals.
There are rides and games for the children.

for this celebration. In Muslim countries, the Id festival lasts for three days. It is a national holiday. In the United States and Canada, Muslims take a day off from work. Their children are allowed to miss a day of school.

Everywhere there is laughter, celebrating, and good food. There are many meat and rice dishes cooked with spices and sweets. Each family prepares their favorite foods.

As the celebration ends, Muslims from all over the world are united in their faith. They have celebrated Ramadan just as Muhammad taught. With Id al-Fitr, they have shared food, laughter, and joy. Everyone looks forward to the next Islamic holiday.

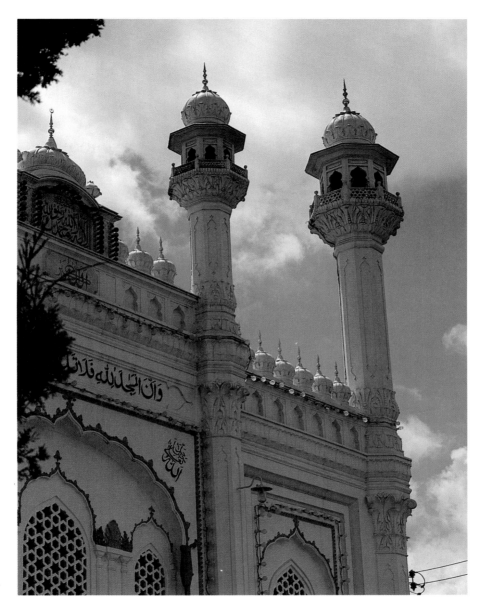

As the celebration ends, Muslims from all over the world are united in their faith.

Glossary

Allah—The Arabic word for God.

ancestors—Family members who are no longer alive.

Arabic—The language of Arab people whose ancestors lived in Arabia.

calligraphy—The art of beautiful writing.

fast—To go without food or water for a certain period of time.

Hafiz—The name given to a person who memorizes the entire Koran.

hajj—The pilgrimage to Mecca that each Muslim must make at least once in his or her lifetime if he or she is in good health and can afford it.

Hegira—Muhammad's flight or escape from Mecca to Medina in the year A.D. 622.

hijab—The scarf that Muslim women and girls wear that covers their head and shoulders.

Id al-Fitr—The festival on the first day of the tenth month following the fast of Ramadan.

iftar—The evening meal eaten after a day of fasting during Ramadan.

imam—The man who leads the prayers in the mosque.

Kaaba—The cubelike building in Mecca that Muslims face toward when praying.

Koran—The Muslim holy book believed to be the actual words of Allah revealed to Muhammad.

mihrab—The alcove in the mosque that shows the direction of Mecca.

minaret—A tower on the mosque from which Muslims are called to prayer.

minbar—A small platform or pulpit in the mosque where someone preaches on Fridays.

mosque—The building where Muslims come to pray and meet with other Muslims.

muezzin—The person who calls the people to prayer from the minaret.

Muslims—People who follow the religion of Islam.

pilgrimage—A long journey to a holy place. Muslims must make the pilgrimage to Mecca at least once.

prophet—A special person who tells others messages from God.

Ramadan—The ninth month of the Islamic calendar.

salat—The duty of all Muslims to pray five times a day.

shahadah—The reciting of the creed or belief of Islam.

suhur—The breakfast eaten before dawn during the month of Ramadan.

sura—A chapter in the Koran.

zakat—The duty of all Muslims to give money to the poor.

Index